OCT -- 2011

JE PARISH
Parish, Herman.
Amelia Bedelia 4 mayor /

P9-EDN-452

$80 \times \frac{1}{20} - W$

Dear Parent:
Your child's love of reading starts here!

Every child learns to read in a different way and at his or her own speed. Some go back and forth between reading levels and read favorite books again and again. Others read through each level in order. You can help your young reader improve and become more confident by encouraging his or her own interests and abilities. From books your child reads with you to the first books he or she reads alone, there are I Can Read Books for every stage of reading:

SHARED READING
Basic language, word repetition, and whimsical illustrations, ideal for sharing with your emergent reader

BEGINNING READING
Short sentences, familiar words, and simple concepts for children eager to read on their own

READING WITH HELP
Engaging stories, longer sentences, and language play for developing readers

READING ALONE
Complex plots, challenging vocabulary, and high-interest topics for the independent reader

ADVANCED READING
Short paragraphs, chapters, and exciting themes for the perfect bridge to chapter books

I Can Read Books have introduced children to the joy of reading since 1957. Featuring award-winning authors and illustrators and a fabulous cast of beloved characters, I Can Read Books set the standard for beginning readers.

A lifetime of discovery begins with the magical words "I Can Read!"

Visit www.icanread.com for information
on enriching your child's reading experience.

I Can Read!

READING
2
WITH HELP

Amelia Bedelia
★ 4 ★
Mayor

story by **Herman Parish**
pictures by **Lynn Sweat**

Alameda Free Library
1550 Oak Street

HarperCollins*Publishers*

Watercolor paints and a black pen were used for the full-color art.

HarperCollins®, ☫®, and I Can Read Book® are trademarks of HarperCollins Publishers.

Amelia Bedelia 4 Mayor Text copyright © 1999 by Herman S. Parish III Illustrations copyright © 1999 by Lynn Sweat All rights reserved. No part of this book may be used or reproduced in any manner whatsoever without written permission except in the case of brief quotations embodied in critical articles and reviews. Manufactured in China. For information address HarperCollins Children's Books, a division of HarperCollins Publishers, 10 East 53rd Street, New York, NY 10022. www.harpercollinschildrens.com

Library of Congress Cataloging-in-Publication Data
Parish, Herman
    Amelia Bedelia 4 mayor / story by Herman Parish ; pictures by Lynn Sweat.
    p.   cm.—(An I can read book)
    Summary: Amelia Bedelia misunderstands what her employer wants her to do, and ends up campaigning for the office of mayor.
    ISBN-10: 0-06-444309-4 (pbk.) — ISBN-13: 978-0-06-444309-8 (pbk.)
    [1. Politics, Practical—Fiction. 2. Household employees—Fiction. 3. Humorous stories.] I. Title: Amelia Bedelia 4 mayor.
II. Sweat, Lynn, ill. III. Title. IV. Series.
PZ7.P2185Am 2001   00-047961
[E]—dc21   CIP
                                                                                                                                    AC

Originally published by Greenwillow Books, an imprint of HarperCollins Publishers, in 1999.
09 10 11 12 13 SCP 20

For Armando and
Angelina Cilenti,
Nonno and Nonna to all
—H.P.

For Ian
—L.S.

"That Mayor Thomas!" said Mr. Rogers.

"What's wrong, dear?" said Mrs. Rogers.

"Mayor Thomas is what's wrong,"
said Mr. Rogers.

"The mayor promised to *cut* taxes.
He never does what he says he will do."

"He is only human," said Mrs. Rogers.
"Besides, no one does exactly
what you tell them to do."

"Here is your breakfast,"
said Amelia Bedelia.
"I hope you like chocolate frosting."
"What is this?" said Mr. Rogers.
"I said I wanted pancakes for breakfast."
"These *are* pan cakes,"
said Amelia Bedelia.
"I baked the cakes in a frying pan.
Do you want to blow out the candles?"
"They are fine," said Mrs. Rogers.
"I will teach you
to make normal pancakes.
You just did what you were told."

"You always do," said Mr. Rogers.

"Why can't Mayor Thomas be like you?

I wish you were the mayor."

"You do?" said Amelia Bedelia.

"Sure," said Mr. Rogers.

"You should run for the mayor's office."

"See you later," said Amelia Bedelia.

She dashed out of the kitchen.

"Where is she going?" said Mrs. Rogers.

"To City Hall!" said Mr. Rogers.

"She *is* running for the mayor's office!"

"I made it!" said Amelia Bedelia.

"Hold on," said the mayor's secretary.

"Mayor Thomas is with the press.

He needs to iron out some things."

"I hate to iron," said Amelia Bedelia.

"I will bring him Mr. Rogers's shirts.

The mayor can press them for me."

She burst into the press conference.

"Amelia Bedelia!" said Mayor Thomas.

"What brings you here?"

"My feet," said Amelia Bedelia.

"I was out running for your office."

"Running for office?" said a reporter.

"The mayor has very big shoes to fill."

"You are rude," said Amelia Bedelia.

"He can't help it if his feet are big."

"You are right," said a reporter.

"Big feet must run in his family."

"How awful," said Amelia Bedelia.

"Don't they ever get to walk?"

All the reporters laughed.

Mayor Thomas did not laugh.

"Ahhhh-CHOOO!" he sneezed.

"His nose runs, too," said a reporter.

"No," said Amelia Bedelia.

"His nose smells."

"I hope his feet don't,"

said a reporter.

"You *are* rude!" said the mayor.

"Amelia Bedelia," asked a reporter,
"what would you do
if you were in the mayor's shoes?"
"I would polish them,"
said Amelia Bedelia.
"They could use a good shine."

Mr. Rogers arrived out of breath.

"Amelia Bedelia, let's go home.

I was joking. You can't run for office."

"I just did," said Amelia Bedelia.

"I always do what folks say to do."

"That is a great promise to make,"

said a reporter.

"I make promises, too," said the mayor.

"We know, we know," said Mr. Rogers.

"But if Amelia Bedelia were mayor . . ."

"You must be joking,"

said Mayor Thomas.

"Amelia Bedelia can't be the mayor."

"I would vote for her," said a reporter.

"We need some change."

"Here's 43 cents," said Amelia Bedelia.

"That's all the change I've got."

"Wait a minute," said the mayor.

"I want to put in my two cents."

"How nice," said Amelia Bedelia.

"That makes 45 cents."

"No, no, no," said the mayor.

" 'My two cents' means 'my opinion.'

I don't really have two cents."

"You don't?" said Amelia Bedelia.

"Then you should get some cents."

"Mayor Thomas doesn't have any sense?" asked a reporter.

"Is that what you just said?"

"No, *he* said that," said Amelia Bedelia.

"I did not!" said the mayor.

"I said I don't have two *pennies*."

"Me neither," said Mr. Rogers.

"I hope Mayor Bedelia cuts taxes."

"*Mayor* Bedelia!" yelled Mayor Thomas.

"She couldn't even be the dog catcher!"

"Yes, I could!" said Amelia Bedelia.

"Take back what you just said!"

"I will not!"

said the mayor.

"Run for mayor," said a reporter.

"Throw your hat in the ring."

"What ring?" said Amelia Bedelia.

The mayor's telephone rang.

Amelia Bedelia took off her hat.

She threw it across the room.

Her hat landed on top of the phone.

"How's that?" said Amelia Bedelia.

"I threw my hat *on* the ring.

Now I can run for mayor."

Amelia Bedelia crouched down.

"On your mark, get set, GO!"

"Hooray!" shouted everyone—

everyone except Mayor Thomas.

A VOTE FOR ME IS A VOTE FOR THE FUTURE!

The race for mayor was on.

Amelia Bedelia

and Mayor Thomas

ran all over town

to talk with the voters.

A VOTE FOR ME IS A VOTE FOR AMELIA BEDELIA!

People began to care more
about their town,
about each other, and their future.

Mr. Rogers gave Amelia Bedelia
lots of help and plenty of good advice.
"Yikes!" said Mr. Rogers.
"Gotcha," said Amelia Bedelia.
"Here's that pole you told me to get."

"Not a fishing pole," said Mr. Rogers.

"What you need is a *voting poll*.

It tells how voters plan

to cast their votes."

"Cast votes?" asked Amelia Bedelia.

"Sounds like fishing to me."

"Most voters are sitting on the fence,"
said Mr. Rogers.

"And you know what that means."

"Sore bottoms," said Amelia Bedelia.

"*Not* sore bottoms," said Mr. Rogers.

"It means people

haven't made up their minds.

This election isn't sewn up yet."

"Hold my pole," said Amelia Bedelia.

"I'll go get a needle and thread.

I will sew it up."

"Forget about sewing and fishing,"

said Mr. Rogers.

"Go out and get some more votes."

Amelia Bedelia walked to town.

A crowd was at the new bridge.

"When I cut this ribbon," said the mayor,

"this brand-new bridge will be open!"

Amelia Bedelia stepped in front of him.

She cut that red ribbon before he did.

"What have you done!" said the mayor.

"Cut that red tape," said Amelia Bedelia

"Everyone says I should get rid
of red tape."

"This is an outrage!" said the mayor.

"You wrecked my photo opportunity."

"Are you having your picture taken?"
said Amelia Bedelia.

"Then you really should smile!"

"That does it!" shouted the mayor.

"I challenge you to a debate!

People will know where I stand."

"I can tell them

where you are standing,"

said Amelia Bedelia.

"On my foot! Owwwwwie!"

On the day of the debate,

the town square was packed.

"Now, let's welcome the mayor

and Amelia Bedelia!"

said the announcer.

Everyone clapped and cheered.

"I am nervous," said Amelia Bedelia.

"Just be yourself," said Mrs. Rogers.

"I always am," said Amelia Bedelia.

"Who else would I be?"

Mr. and Mrs. Rogers each gave her

a big hug.

The mayor and Amelia Bedelia
argued for hours.

"I will fill in all the potholes,"
said Mayor Thomas.

"Me, too," said Amelia Bedelia.

"You can't cook in pots with holes."

"That's silly," said the mayor.

"It sure is," said Amelia Bedelia.

"All the food falls out."

"That's right!" yelled the crowd.

"I will reduce the school tax,"
said Mayor Thomas.

"And I won't," said Amelia Bedelia.

"Our schools need more tacks.

Especially thumbtacks."

"You tell him!" shouted the crowd.

"My goodness!" said Mrs. Rogers.

"They are fighting like cats and dogs."

HI-SSST! BOW-WOW-WOW!

A big dog chased a cat across the stage.

Mayor Thomas rescued the cat.

Amelia Bedelia grabbed the dog.

"Good job!" said Mayor Thomas.

"You mean that?" said Amelia Bedelia.

"I sure do," said Mayor Thomas.

"You proved that you can be

the dog catcher. I take back what I said.

I apologize to you."

"I accept your apology,"

said Amelia Bedelia.

"And now I can stop running for mayor."

"No! Don't quit!" shouted the crowd.

"Listen to me," said Amelia Bedelia.

"I said I would run for mayor *unless* Mayor Thomas took back what he said. He took it back.

So now I don't have to run any more."

No one moved or made a sound.

"I admire you," said the mayor.

"You know how to keep a promise."

He began to clap for Amelia Bedelia.

Then the whole crowd joined in.

"Good news," said Mr. Rogers.

"The mayor kept his promise."

"See there," said Mrs. Rogers.

"You *can* teach an old dog new tricks."

"I don't have time," said Amelia Bedelia

"And I am *not* catching any more dogs.

I am going to the White house."

"The White House!" said Mr. Rogers.

"You are going to Washington?"

"Of course not," said Amelia Bedelia.

"I borrowed a book from Mrs. White.

She said to leave it at her house."

"Whew!" said Mr. Rogers.

"I thought

you were running for president!"

"I will do whatever you say,"

said Amelia Bedelia.

Mr. Rogers did not say one more word . .

even when he got his French toast.

ALAMEDA FREE LIBRARY

Read all the books about
Amelia Bedelia

Amelia Bedelia
by Peggy Parish
pictures by Fritz Siebel

Thank You, Amelia Bedelia
by Peggy Parish
pictures by Barbara Siebel Thomas

Amelia Bedelia and the Surprise Shower
by Peggy Parish
pictures by Barbara Siebel Thomas

Come Back, Amelia Bedelia
by Peggy Parish
pictures by Wallace Tripp

Play Ball, Amelia Bedelia
by Peggy Parish
pictures by Wallace Tripp

Teach Us, Amelia Bedelia
by Peggy Parish
pictures by Lynn Sweat

Good Work, Amelia Bedelia
by Peggy Parish
pictures by Lynn Sweat

Amelia Bedelia Helps Out
by Peggy Parish
pictures by Lynn Sweat

Amelia Bedelia and the Baby
by Peggy Parish
pictures by Lynn Sweat

Amelia Bedelia Goes Camping
by Peggy Parish
pictures by Lynn Sweat

Merry Christmas, Amelia Bedelia
by Peggy Parish
pictures by Lynn Sweat

Amelia Bedelia's Family Album
by Peggy Parish
pictures by Lynn Sweat

Good Driving, Amelia Bedelia
by Herman Parish
pictures by Lynn Sweat

Bravo, Amelia Bedelia!
by Herman Parish
pictures by Lynn Sweat

Amelia Bedelia 4 Mayor
by Herman Parish
pictures by Lynn Sweat

Calling Doctor Amelia Bedelia
by Herman Parish
pictures by Lynn Sweat

Amelia Bedelia, Bookworm
by Herman Parish
pictures by Lynn Sweat

Happy Haunting, Amelia Bedelia
by Herman Parish
pictures by Lynn Sweat

Amelia Bedelia, Rocket Scientist?
by Herman Parish
pictures by Lynn Sweat

Amelia Bedelia Under Construction
by Herman Parish
pictures by Lynn Sweat

Herman Parish

was in the fourth grade when his aunt, Peggy Parish, wrote the first book about Amelia Bedelia. The lovable, literal-minded housekeeper has been a member of his family ever since. Peggy Parish died in 1988. She would be proud and delighted to know that her nephew is carrying on Amelia Bedelia with titles including *Good Driving, Amelia Bedelia*; *Bravo, Amelia Bedelia!*; *Amelia Bedelia, Bookworm*; and *Amelia Bedelia, Rocket Scientist?*

Lynn Sweat

has illustrated many Amelia Bedelia books, including *Bravo, Amelia Bedelia!*; *Good Driving, Amelia Bedelia*; *Amelia Bedelia, Bookworm*; and *Amelia Bedelia, Rocket Scientist?* He is a painter as well as an illustrator, and his paintings hang in galleries across the country. He and his wife live in Connecticut.